Bepanah 'Ishq

Flairs and Glairs
Publication House

"Bepanah Ishq"

ISBN No: " 978-93-91302-38-2"
1st Edition
Language – English and Hindi

Flairs and Glairs
Publication House
Regd. Under MSME Act.

Disclaimer

This is a work of fiction and solely represent the thoughts of the corresponding authors of the articles. Our editors have tried their best to edit the content of all the authors and check the plagiarism.

All the write-ups in this book are unique and are only published in this book.

In case any plagiarism or error is found, only the author is responsible alone, and not the publisher or the Compilers.

Cover Designing and Book Formatting
Shubham Shah and Ishani Agarwal

Co Author

Shubham Shah (Founder Flairs and Glairs)
Ishani Agarwal (Founder Flairs and Glairs)

1. Nelofer Talukdar(Compiler)
2. Nilanjana Sarkar
3. Vibhor Bijoy
4. Roopali Purohit
5. Saba Parvez
6. Yashvi Srivastava
7. Yamini Sona Vaishnavi
8. Humsala Sri. R.,
9. Rashika Jain
10. Rashmi Baweja
11. Prachi Gupta
12. Shivani M. R. Joshi
13. Ashwini Kumar Singh
14. Swayamdeepta Das
15. S.Vidhyalakshmi
16. Ankita Jain
17. Urvi Gajjar
18. Vivek Chandra
19. Muskaan Manoj Kumar
20. Avi Srivastava
21. Nikita Mitra
22. Khevana Purohit
23. Riya Srivastava
24. Sriyasri Patra
25. Gurleen Kaur
26. Pragya Verma
27. Suprabhat
28. Padma Srivastava
29. Rajveer Atal

30. S. Saraswetha
31. Jacob Rosario
32. Sona Agarwal
33. Krishna Motwani
34. Monisha. T
35. Kathijathul Kubra. R
36. Yasmin S
37. Lena. M
38. Dhruvi Dhariwal
39. Sofiya Mehake N
40. Kowsalya Thangadurai
41. Sujish Kandampully
42. Yash Ojha
43. Pragyan Panda
44. Diksha Motwani
45. Nihal M Jagirdar
46. Jata_V
47. Japsimran Kaur
48. Pratham Mittal
49. Ruma Begam
50. Ipsita Panigrahi
51. Smriti Srivastava

Shubham Shah

(Founder- Flairs and Glairs)

Shubham Shah, an entrepreneur at "Flairs & Glairs" a brand with dynamics in events organizing and cultural educational pan INDIA, is a 26yrs old guy who recently has entered the digital platform of imprinting emotions. He has initiated with his own open mic platform to help budding poets and aspiring writers under his brand named as "Teekhe Zasbaaat"

He is a commerce graduate from the Bhagalpur City of Bihar.

He states Writing has impersonated him since childhood and he has now been writing for over a decade!

Cooking, on the other hand, is his passion! He also mentions, trying out new things just tickles him!

When asked sir, Why SPICY EMOTIONS?

He smiled and added, "agar jasbaat teekhe na ho toh wo jasbaat kahan" Spices are all that blends! So do his words!

As a chef, he presents to you his dish! Hot and freshly served! Taste it! Feel it! Enjoy it! You can also find his writing in the Book "Teekhe Zasbaaat" and 50+ Co-authored anthologies. With his passion to explore opportunities across Platforms, he is working with keen devotion and We wish him all the very best for his future ventures.

He is Featured in the International Magazine DeMode for his upcoming solo novel.

He is Approved by Ne8x for its Lit Fest, and is a Golden Star Awards 2020 Winner.

He is a India Book of Records Holder for his Anthology Satrang, and has the Grandmaster title by Asia Book of Records, for the same.

He has also been featured in Prabhat Khabar, Dainik Jagran, and a lot of other Newspapers in Bihar for his achievements.

He has been a proud co-author to

India Book Of Records (Title- Black)

World Book Of Records (Title -15 Wonders of Poetries)

India Book Of Records (Title - Aaina)

Vajra World Records Holder (Title - Gustakhi Maaf Hai)

High Range of Records Holder (Title - Gustakhi Maaf Hai)

Indian Book of Records

(Title - Road from Worst to Best)

Share your reviews on his

@spicy_emotions
@shubham4shah
Or via email on
shubham2shah@gmail.com

To stay tuned to his work and opportunities follow his business Handles

INSTAGRAM   FACEBOOK   YOUTUBE

@flairsandglairs
@teekhezasbaaat

WEBSITE:

https://flairsandglairs.in/
https://flairsandglairs.com/

Ishani Agarwal

(Co-Founder- Flairs and Glairs)

Ishani Agarwal hails from the City of Joy, Kolkata.
She is the co-founder of her Community "Teekhe Zasbaaat" and Flairs and Glairs Publication.
Been a Compiler for 45+ Anthologies, she is in the process for more. Co-authored in 150+ Anthologies. She is a India Book of Records Holder, a Vajra World Records Holder, a High Range of Records Holder, an OMG Book of Records Holder, a Bravo Record holder, a Forever Star Book of World Records and an Indian Book of Records Holder.
Approved by Ne8x for its Lit Fest 2020, and Literary Icon 2020. Also a Golden Star Awards Winner 2020.
She has also been awarded with India Star Republic Award 2021, a part of She Awards by Awards Arc and Winner of Nari Samman 2021 by Literoma.

She is also selected as Best Achiever of the Year by AwardsArc and Most Challenging Compiler Award by Spectrum Awards.
She got her first solo Published,a solo Compilation consisting of first 750 contents of hers, titled "Hand That Burnt While Healing".

She has been featured by the National Magazine "Taree Zameen Par" with the title 'unstoppable'.
Also featured in the International Magazine DeMode for her upcoming solo novel, she is proud to write on social issues, and is happy with the love she is receiving.
Connect with her on Instagram: @Ishani_agarwal_quotes / @compilations_so_far

NELOFER TALUKDAR
(Compiler)

Nelofer Talukdar born in 2000, and brought up in the capital city of the abode of clouds, Shillong. She has also been a part of 18+ anthologies. She is working as a Ambassador in WYIMUN India. Her biggest dream is to be the reason behind bringing a bright and everlasting smile on her father's face. She also wants to be a good writer. And aspires to become a defence officer in the near future and work for her mother land.

Instagram Handle: talukdar__shruti

Your quote– Nelofer Talukdar

Bepanah ishq
Bepanah ishq hai tumse
Bepanah ishq hai tumse
Chahe tum mujhse bahut dur kyon na ho
Par ishq tumse hi hai

Ajnabi
"Hum ajnabi the
Ha hum ajnabi the....
Phir ajnabi se dost hue.
Phir dost se aashiq hue.
Aashiq se phir ajnabi hogaye...
Aur ye sab safar dekha hai maine...
Ishq ko dosti par chup chup kar haste hue dekha hai mai
ne"...

NILANJANA SARKAR

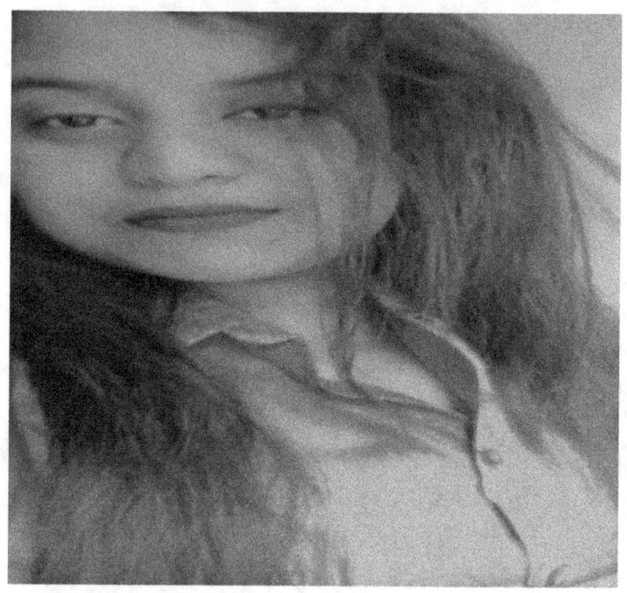

This is Nilanjana Sarkar. She hails from West Bengal, Alipurduar and currently she's studying in class 12 and working as a head of the Publication in WYIMUN on based on the three committee WHO, UNHRC and UNDP. She is very hardworking and passionate girl and loves to do creativity through her writing, she mostly writes on erotics stuffs as well as on many topics which helps her to explore her more and more. She is a public speaker as well as a motivational speaker. She is an impulsive writer who oozes out her emotions and feelings and thoughts via writing. She has a good working experience with many eminent personalities across the globe.

Wo log, Bohot khush kismat the
Wo log, Bohot khush kismat the
Jo ishq ko kaam samjhte the,
Ya kaamse aashiqui rakhte the
Jo ishq ko kam samjhte the,
Ya kaamse aashiqui rakhte the
Ham jeete jee mashroof rahe gaye...
Kuch ishq kiya, kuch mashroof kiya,
Kaam ishq ke aare aata raha
Aur ishq se kaam ulajhta raha...
Kaam ishq ke aare aata raha
Aur ishq se kaam ulajhta raha...
Fir akhir tang akar hamne
Dono ko hi adhura chor diya.

Nahi ho mere kabil
Tumhe ye bhi pata hai...
Nahi ho mere kabil
Tumhe ye bhi pata hai...
Waqt k sath sath
Pyaar tumhara hi ghata hai...
Nahi ho tum kabil mere
Nahi ho tum kabil mere...
Ab hazar reason lekar
Mere samne mat aana...
Haqiket to door ki baat hai
Tum toh meri khawabo mebhi mat aana...
Insaan hi rehne dena mujhe
An khuda mat bana dena...

VIBHOR BIJOY

Vibhor Bijoy is a software engineer by profession and a poet by passion. He loves to jot down his feelings in a candid manner
He has been a part of various amazing anthologies.

एक नज़र

सोचता हू की आपकी एक नज़र का दीदार हम करते तो
बंदिशों की ज़ंजीरो को तोड़ देते
सोचता हू की आपकी एक नज़र की झलक मिलती तो सोई हुई
किस्मत के जागरण से मनहूसियत के रावण का संघार हम करते
सोचता हू की आपकी एक नज़र हम पर पड़ती तो खुदखुशी के
वायरस को हम साहस के एंटीबाडी से ठीक करते
सोचता हूँ की आपकी एक नज़र के दर्शन से हम सदियों से भरे
ग़म के रेगिस्तान में हम खुशियों की हरियाली ला देते
सोचता हूँ की आपकी एक नज़र का दीदार हम करते तो अनकहे
अलफ़ाज़ से आपका दिल खुशनुमा कर देते
आपकी एक नज़र मिलती तो वो दिल की जुबां बना देते
दिल की जुबां बना देते!!

ROOPALI PUROHIT

Roopali is an ambivert who loves to weave stories in her head.
Weaving those stories and making them live on paper is her hobby and passion both.

Arranged love.

He entered his room, anticipating after all the pomp and show they were finally alone as a man and wife and with just two meetings they weren't even sure about each other's hobby and spending life with a stranger was exciting yet scary.

He saw her in casual attire, her clothes in his wardrobe made much sense and he felt a surge of possessiveness pass through him.

"You can use the left side of the bed"

"So you are ordering and assuming already aren't you."

His cheeks turned red and he was embarrassed he never wanted to make her uncomfortable, he was about to apologize but he saw her sheepish expression and in that moment he felt love pass through his body mind and soul.

SABA PARVEZ

A fervent writer who knows how to pen down her sentiments on those deadpan sheets!

Insta Id:- @deperilme

Nigah-e-shauq se jo yun,
Nagma-e-ulfat dohrate ho...
Mehek uthti hai khwabgah bhi,
Jab dastan-e-mohabbat sunate ho...

Khamoshi se be-laus bazm-e-anjum,
Aur be-khud mohabbat mein dube hum...
Cigarette ki rakh se bhari ash tray,
Aur teri yaadon ka ehsaas-e-gam...

Laut pade the wapas samt-e-safar mein be-dast-o-paa,
Tere chaab se hi teri ana ka meyaar karke...
Mashgul rehne ki koshish mein uljhe rahe har chashm-e-zadan,
Kambakht sukoon aya bhi toh year deedar karke...

Aaj phir neendein ojhal hain nigahoon se,
Khayaloon ke shor mein khamoshi ko sunn na hoga...
Aaj phir tishnagi ke daman mein lipat kar,
Gam-e-shikastagi ko chunn na hoga...

YASHVI SRIVASTAVA

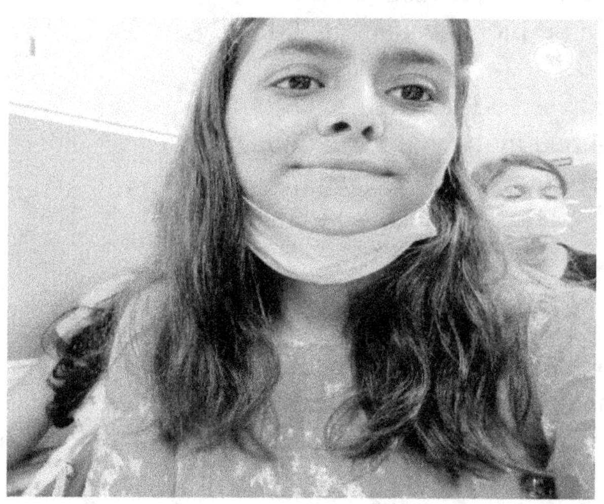

Yashvi Srivastava

You
Everyday spent with you was a memory,
Man i love you!
I don't know what I should do to make you stay!
I don't know what's next.
But it's all gonna hurt!
I love you hon

I miss you
There without you or with you won't matter as long as we are connected with hearts and souls. I remember how you used to write me long paragraphs on how much you loved me. It's all here; the paragraphs; the memories; and most specifically, "me".
The only thing that changed is you and time.
Well let it be!
I can live without you but i don't want to.
I miss you...

YAMINI SONA VAISHNAVI

Yamini Sona Vaishnavi is a student of English Literature who pursues her III year in Madurai, Tamil Nadu. She loves to play with words and she has a great passion for writing, especially poetry. She is already a co-author for 10 anthologies. She wishes to pour down her emotions in the form of poetry so that it will reach the hearts of the readers.

The past- life memory:

I was too young to know the literal meaning of friendship...
Yet, I had a very big crew who were naughty just like me even though I was new...
I treated all the same, but I had one pal who treated me differently...
I heard she lost her sister a year back and now smiles after a really long time...
She was just a friend to me, but I was someone more than others to her...
Even when I absented for the daily games, she would arrive at my house...
She was so caring yet her attitude towards me was mysterious...
I took half a year to analyze her character to find out a concealed truth...
To completely know what was hidden but she never uttered a word...
One day, she came to me, walking with her little tootsie...
She said "I love you more and thank you!"...
I confused and was taken aback when she told me "Thanks for saving me in my past life! I was your close friend just like how we are now together! , I know you won't trust me, because you were the same even in your past life ...with skeptical mind, loads of care and unlimited love!"
I didn't wish to sense the reality but I sensed her love towards me....

HUMSALA SRI R., MDGA., MCA.,

This is Humsala Sri who is just 21yr old girl daughter of Raveendran from Ramanathapuram district doing MCA, she used to write quotes and lines based on love, inspiration and many more, she used to motivate others and keep a positive vibes around.

Love is a beautiful feeling which emerges from the core of our heart. Nobody can find any kind of theory or logic as how love generates, when it is generated etc. It is a feeling which is unconditional, be it the relationship of child with his parents, friends, relatives and other people.

One of the purest forms of emotions that human beings are capable of exhibiting is the emotion of love. The love we have for others and the love that we have for ourselves are both interrelated in most cases.

A human being will be inconsiderate in loving someone if he or she does not love themselves in the first place.

Religion teaches us to spread love and peace amongst our fellow men on the planet but it is people with narrow line of thinking that they assume that love has conditions and is limited to a specific section of culture and ethnicity.

RASHIKA JAIN

She is a pursuasive writer.
She loves to travel, cook and dance.
She believes her to be a soul at peace.
She is extremely optimistic and spiritual by heart and mind.

I Am Ready To Heal

On the loneliest night that I could feel,
Looking for peace and ready to heal.
I drive my way to the endless skies
Hitting a convo with the moon and stars nearby.
I could never get a company better than this,
For I have got the most beautiful, nature's bliss.
I can talk all night fearless,
For I know they won't judge my intentions, more or less.
The moon is eager to unlock my reality,
Stars are too showering me with love despite me being silly.
I feel so warm, I feel so good.
I have got the best company, the stars and the moon.

RASHMI BAWEJA

रश्मी इस कहानी की लेखिका बिल्कुल अपने नाम के अनुरूप ही सबके जीवन को प्रकाशित करती है। रश्मी हरियाणा के सोनीपत जिले की निवासी है। उन्होंने MCA किया है। उन्होंने अपना लेखन कार्य 2016 में प्रारंभ किया। वे बहुत ही स्पष्ट वादी है।वे फेसबुक पर HEART TOUCHING पेज पर भी लिखती हैंlhttps://www.facebook.com/rashmibaweja1993/अलग अलग विषयों पर वे बहुत अच्छा लिखती हैं। उनकी रचनाएँ पढ़कर दिल को सुकून मिलता है। दूसरों के मनोभावों को वे बखूबी समझती हैं। अपने अनुभवों व दूसरों को समझने के अपने हुनर के आधार पर ही वे अपनी रचना लेकर आई हैं। उन्हें इसके लिए बहुत बधाई। आशा है कि उनकी ये रचना सभी को बहुत पसंद आएगी और वे भविष्य में भी ऐसे ही लिखती रहेगी।

बेपनाह इश्क़

ज़िन्दगी का हर पल हम तेरे साथ बिताना चाहते थे।
हम तुझे अपनी पलको पर बिठाना चाहते थे।
फिर क्यों तू मुझे इस क़दर बीच मझदार में छोड़ गया।
हम तो अपना बेपनाह इश्क़ तुझसे निभाना चाहते थे।।

दुनिया की नज़र से चुराकर तुझे अपने दिल मे बसाना चाहते थे।
हम तो तुझे खुदा से भी बढ़कर मानते थे।
फिर क्या कमी थी मेरी मोहब्बत में जो तूने किसी और का हाथ थामा।
हम तो अपना बेपनाह इश्क़ तुझसे निभाना चाहते थे।।

हम तो तुझे अपनी किस्मत की लकीरों में लिखवाना चाहते थे।
ज़िन्दगी में तेरे गम लेकर तेरे साथ खुशिया बाटना चाहते थे।
फिर क्यों तूने मुझे ही गमो के अंधेरे में धकेल दिया।
हम तो अपना बेपनाह इश्क़ तुझसे निभाना चाहते थे।।

तेरे लिए तो हम खुदा से भी लड़ना जानते थे।
तू साथ तो देता हम तो तेरा हाथ थामकर चलना चाहते थे।
फिर क्यों तूने बिना कुछ बताए रास्ते अलग कर लिए।
हम तो अपना बेपनाह इश्क़ तुझसे निभाना चाहते थे।।

हम तो अपनी हर मुराद में बस तेरा साथ मांगते थे।
तेरे किये तो हम खुदा से भी रूठ जाया करते थे।
फिर तू क्यों इस कदर रूठकर मुझसे दूर चला गया।
हम तो अपना बेपनाह इश्क़ तुझसे निभाना चाहते थे।।

तुम्हारे साथ के बिना
तुम्हारे पास होने से मुझे मेरा जीवन पूरा लगता है।
तेरे साथ से मुझे मेरी हर मुश्किल का हल मिलता है।
अनजाने सफर में तेरा विश्वास मेरी हिम्मत बनता है।
तुम्हारे साथ के बिना मुझे मेरे जीवन अधूरा लगता है।।

तुम्हारा मुझे मिल जाना अब तक सपना सा लगता है।
तेरा मेरे रिश्तो को संभाल कर रखना मेरा दिल छूता है।
कैसे बयाँ कर सकता हूँ मैं तेरे प्यार को कुछ शब्दों में।
तुम्हारे साथ के बिना मुझे मेरे जीवन अधूरा लगता है।।

तेरा चेहरा देखने से मेरा हर सवेरा खूबसूरत लगता है।
तू अपनी चमक से मेरे पूरे दिन को रोशन करता है।
कैसे बताऊँ मैं तुझे तेरी अहमियत अपनी ज़िन्दगी में।
तुम्हारे साथ के बिना मुझे मेरे जीवन अधूरा लगता है।।

तेरा हर सफर में मेरे साथ चलना मेरी हिम्मत बढ़ाता है।
तेरा हाथ थामना मेरे रुके हुए कदमो में जान डालता है।
तू खुद का दिया हुआ मेरी ज़िन्दगी का सबसे खूबसूरत तोहफा है।
तुम्हारे साथ के बिना मुझे मेरे जीवन अधूरा लगता है।।

तू मेरे सपनों में रोज़ उम्मीद के नए नए रंग भरता है।
मेरे सपनों को पूरा करने के लिये तू मुझसे भी लड़ता है।
तूने मेरे सपनों को अपना सपना बनाकर जिया है।
तुम्हारे साथ के बिना मुझे मेरे जीवन अधूरा लगता है।।

PRACHI GUPTA

Prachi Gupta is a Vivacious and kind-hearted girl who hails from Allahabad, UP and she loves to scribble her random thoughts and imagination on a blank canvas. Beside this, she is hardworking Digital Marketer and a moddy compiler who has compiled an anthology named "The Harrowing Heart" as well as a Co-Author of many anthologies.

Can Follow her on Instagram for more updates:-
@_prachi_gupta_210
@prachigupta3435

If, I Care

Yes, I know I don't miss you
Yes, I know I don't talk to you
Yes, even I know...
I don't like to meet-up with you.

Yes, I don't look at you
But, I care for you a lot

Yes, I don't show it to you
But, I adore you so much
But, you don't want to know

Yes, I know I don't call you
But, what?
If, I care to call you
Don't you know that?
I love you too.

SHIVANI M. R. JOSHI

She is Shivani M.R. Joshi. She is from Ahmedabad, Gujarat and 20yrs old. She's a teacher by profession and a student too. She started developing interest in writing during lockdown (19/5/2020) and slowly slowly started participating in anthologies and computation. Dedicated to an mix. Currently she's working as a project manager in Priun publications and project head in sunshine. She had wrote several write up anthologies and it created a passion in herself and it's her dream to become a doctor in future.

म्होब्बत भी क्या चीज है

मोहब्बत भी बड़ी कमाल की चीज है
सुकून भी यही और तन्हाई भी यही है
दर्द भी यही और दवाई भी यही है
हंसी भी यही और उदासी भी यही है
जिंदगी भी यही और मौत भी यही है...

ASHWINI KUMAR SINGH

He is Ashwini Singh, a budding pharmacist from Delhi . He has been writing quotes and poems since long back but never thought of writing them for publication purpose. It is due to his friend that he has entered in this field. He is very thankful to his friend.

The Unbreakable Bond...

Strong like a Hydrogen bond,
Flexible like a rubber,
As thin like a thread,
As deep as river,
This is my love for you dear...
As precious like a diamond,
As speedy like time,
As busy as a bee,
In my life,
This is totally lost me...
Thinking about you gives me break,
That moment is like delicious cake,
I love to get lost in those feelings,
As those moments are quite healing...
But busy schedule is our greatest enemy,
It hates your and my unity,
It keeps us separately,
Just like two banks of river,
Which are with each other,
But parallel...
Without each other,
We are incomplete,
We may have differences,
But similarities have importance...
Our bond has grown stronger,
Our interest has deepened,
Issues will remain there,
But I believe we will stay together...
Just because our bonds are
REALLY INSEPARABLE...

SWAYAMDEEPTA DAS

She is Swayamdeepta Das, residing in Hindmotor,a suburban town in Hooghly district of West Bengal. She has passed class 12 from Vivekananda Academy and will pursue engineering.She loves music, sketching and is an ardent reader of crime fiction. She is a co-author of 57+ anthologies. She is a realistic person. She has also compiled and edited a book 'Pure Bliss' which is going to be published soon. Instagram-swayamdeepta_das

Books and movies, two amazing ways
Of passing time and rejuvenating mind
But what is the difference?
Books don't strain our eyes the way movies do.
That's a health benefit we cannot deny
But there are aesthetic reasons for preferring books
They give us the opportunity to visualize
The incidents and characters we read
It boosts our imagination
Unlike movies which serve everything before our eyes
As we create the image of the story in our mind,
We are transported to a different world
Which gives us an unknown pleasure?
Books always provide us knowledge
Which we may not gain from every movie
Movies showcase violence and other evils
Which tempt the young generation to stray away from the right path?
But books mostly teach us to distinguish between right and wrong.

S. VIDHYALAKSHMI

She is S. Vidhyalakshmi from Tamilnadu, Cuddalore. She has completed her Post graduation in English and.., she is a translator, critic and the language trainer too.. Her passion towards reading is prompted her to write..
She strongly believes,
"Be yourself everyone else is taken"
            -Oscar Wilde
So, she is her only inspiration..!
Insta I'd: vidhyasampath98.

Broken love...
Dear Love.,
You are the one...
Who changed my life?
From.
Hardship to happiness,
Failure to succeed,
Dark to brighten,
Solitary to sociable,
You have given me
"Unshakable hope"
Only you deserve to
Share my soul...
Finally,
You broke my heart and left...
But,
You can feel my innocent love
In midst of my
BROKEN HEART...

ANKITA JAIN

मेरा अब तक का सफ़र

ये बात उसकी है जो बहुत महत्वकांशी है। उसकी अभिलाषा हमेशा से कुछ अलग करने की रही है। पर उस ने हमेशा कुछ और ही करने में अपना समय निकाल दिया। अब जीवन के तीस वर्ष निकल गए थे तब वह एक पत्नी, बहु,और एक माँ की जिम्मेदारी निभा रही थी। वो फिर से अपनी पहचान बनाने की कोशिश कर रही थी। शादी के पहले उसने इंजीनियरिंग की पढ़ाई पूरी कर के अच्छी कंपनी में नौकरी की थी। ग्रहणी होने के साथ साथ वो अपने जीवन में एक सकारात्मक परिवर्तन करना चाहती है। अब उस ओर बढ़ रही है। वो अपने को ऊंचे मक़ाम पर देखना चाहती है।

मोहब्बत होती है दिलों के मिलने से
दिल मिलते हैं जज़्ज़बात कि आहट से
जज़्ज़बात जब एक जैसे होते है
तब इश्क़ का सूरूर चढ़ता है
प्यार अपने मुक़ाम को पाने आगे बढ़ता है
न मिले मंज़िल तो बेगुनाह को सज़ा होती है
इश्क़ मुश्किल में और प्यार बेपनाह होता है

बेपरवाह इंसान को प्यार की कद्र कहाँ
हमनवां न बनें उसे किसी की जरूरत कहाँ
उनके इज़हार के बिना हमारा प्यार अधूरा है
उनके इक़रार बिना हमारा इश्क़ बेपनाह है

URVI GAJJAR

Born in Maharashtra (Mumbai), Urvi Gajjar is a 21 years old young author, graduated in commerce. Her innovative ideas, loving heart and the enthusiasm towards literature brimmed her personality with the shining pearls of beautiful sayings. She says, "If i have waited for perfection, i could have never written a word". She takes writing as an art and that art has enabled her to create many books to her credits as a co author. The names are

Hey, I am sorry"   "Golden times"   "Khud rang"
"Poetaster-life of poet"   "Adonic story"

"Mid night conversation" "Proposal to poetry" "Moons and stars" and many more yet to publish

Right now, she is working on her own Anthology "A Game of Dice" expected to be released soon.

She dedicates all her success to her mother MRS. ILA GAJJAR and her brother MR. HARSH GAJJAR.

You can contact her in Instagram at @urvi_gajjar_

(or) Through mail: urvigajjar1234@gmail.com

Love

Love is when you can feel the person without actually touching them

Love is when you hug the person and smell the person and you blush

Love is when you can't see them sad and can u every possible thing to make them happy

Love is when you can pretend to be happy just because you don't want the person to be sad cause of you

Love is when after a long fight just a smile just a hug or just giggling is enough rather than expensive gifts

Love is when you can be childish and do lot of masti but no one will judge you

Love is when you are sick the person take care of you so much that nobody can

Love is when you can just not meet for days, weeks or years but still it won't be faded

Love is when you can trust the person so blindly that you can play "Trust fall" game also without any hesitation

Love is when you don't be selfish and you think of the person first then u think about yourself

Love is when fight is going on you just not say a word not because you don't have anything to say but because you don't want to hurt the person

Love is when you are exhausted and you meet the person you talk to them and all your stress and exhaustion just get waved off

Love is when you miss the person so much and the person appears right in front of you isn't its a miracle

Yes u can say its miracle but for me its an connection between heart to heart its and connection between soul to soul its and connection between person to person

When u love someone you don't see the looks , face structure, speech, skin tone, body, personality, or other things you see is a pure soul the heart of that person mater's not other things

So when you love someone your love should be pure and make that infinity and beyond

All should be like damn they are still together that's Love

VIVEK CHANDRA

वह जीवन के प्रति सकारात्मक नज़रिया रखता है और समाज में असहाय लोगों के प्रति एक चेतना जागृत करना चाहता है,विशेषकर बुजुर्गों के लिए कुछ अच्छा करना चाहता है जिससे हमारे समाज में वृद्धाश्रमों में कमी आए।

Instagram: raahi_09

"तक़दीर लिख दे"

जो रूठ गया है वो हो मेरे पास ऐसी कोई तहरीर लिख दे,
मेरी दास्ताँ-ए-इश्क़ को फिर से मेरी तक़दीर लिख दे।

अश्फ़ाक था जो एकमात्र इस हबीब का...उसे मेरे करीब लिख दे,
हो जाये राहत की बारिश मेरी रूह पर...ऐसी कोई तरक़ीब लिख दे।

गर मैं हूँ क़ातिब तो उसे मेरी किताब लिख दे,
मेरी हर नज़्म में उसका ही ज़िक्र हो...इश्क़ ऐसा बेहिसाब लिख दे।

तेरे जहाँ में ख़ालिस मेरी गुज़ारिश लिख दे।
पनाह दे ऐ मालिक अब तो अपनी नवाज़िश लिख दे।

तारीक का मंज़र है चारों तरफ...अब तो ज़िया से वाक़िफ़ लिख दे,
हर मर्ज़ से करा दिया है वाकिफ़...अब दवा का भी नाफ़िज़ लिख दे।

ए ख़ुदा भले मुझ पर जहाँ के सारे नालिश लिख दे,
मुकम्मल कर दूँ हर ख़्वाहिश..गर तू ख़्वाब-ए-नर्गिस लिख दे।

भले ही इसे मेरे दर्द की नुमाइश लिख दे या मेरे ज़ख़्मों की पैमाइश लिख दे।
उसे ही मेरी पहली और आख़री ख़्वाहिश लिख दे।।

MUSKAAN MANOJ KUMAR

Muskaan Manoj Kumar, a 19 year old girl, currently pursuing 2nd year Media and Communication in Manipal Academy of Higher Education Dubai UAE. She is passionate about dancing, her hobbies are singing, writing and reading. She loves her family and friends.

Bepanah ishq ki dastaan
Har ek mohabbat Bepanah hoti hai chahe woh kisi seh bhi ho. Mera pyaar bhi bepanah tha mai apne partner seh baahut pyaar karti thi woh bhi bepanah ishq wala, kisiki parwah nahi karti thi. Uske liye sabkuch karti thi. Hamara pyaar bepanah tha par uske taraf seh woh ishq dheere dheere kam hota gaya. Ab uske taraf seh woh bepanah ishq nahi raha. Mai abhi bhi usse pehle ki tarah aur zyaada pyaar karne lagi thi. Usne mujhe dhoka kahin baar diya tha phir bhi maine woh sab undekha kiya. Jaise bolte hai na ki pyaar andha hota hai yeh baat toh sahi hai. Har baare Mai yeh sochti thi ki aaj nahi toh Kal sab theek hojayega akhir kab tak woh dhoka dega kabhi toh mujhse wapas pyaar karega. Yeh san mere bepanah ishq ka saboot tha kyunki Mai kuch nahi khuch dekh rahi thi. But baad mai samaj aaya ki yeh bepanah ishq kis kaam ka jab john Mera partner hai usko mujse pyaar nahi. Toh mai ek baate kahungi bepanah ishq karna sahi hai par unse joh uske layak ho. Unse nahi john layak hi na ho.

AVI SRIVASTAVA

He is an engineering student aimed to make his name in computer world.... Poetry is not only is his hobby but also a way to express his feelings....
Instagram Id: Avishri99

साथ हमारा.....

हसीन लम्हो का पिटारा था वो साथ हमारा....
वो नाव की सवारी और अस्सी घाट का किनारा....
वो छिप के मिलना और गोलगप्पो पे गुजारा....
तुम न हो साथ मेरे बस इन यादों का हैं सहारा....

बदला था मैंने शहर बस, जज़्बात मेरे आज भी वहीं हैं....
चाहे छोड़ चुकी हैं साथ मेरा, फिर भी वो मुझमें बाकी कहीं हैं....
दूरी की वजह से थोड़ा, नही दे पाया उसे मैं वक्त....
अब बिन उसके जियूँ या बहा लूँ अपना रक्त...

वो तेरा आना...

छत पर तेरा यूँ रोज कपड़े सुखाना....
देख मुझे शर्मा कर छुप जाना....
मेरा रोज कसरत के बहाने तुझे निहारना....
बयां न कर सकता मेरे जीवन मे तेरा आना....

वो तेरे छत पर जान कर पतंग गिरना....
कागज के जहाज पर दिल की बातें लिखना....
अनजाना सा हैं ये एहसास मुश्किल हैं तम्हें समझाना....
तेरा तोलिये से बारिशें आज़ाद करना करे मुझे दीवाना....

NIKITA MITRA

Myself Nikita Mitra hailing from Assam pursuing B.Com.Beside from writing I also love to draw. I started writing since when I was in school and now somewhere it's a part of my life. I'm not a professional writer but I'm on my way to weave the web of my own fate.

Unke baaton se aaj aisa laga,
Nafrat karte hain wo humse behadh,
Bepanah pyaar karne wala bandha,
Aaj fikar tak nhi karta.
Jiske saath rehne ke liye,
Puri duniya se ladhli maine,
Aaj usine akele jeene ka paigaam de diya.
Zindagi ka safar ab akele hi katna hai mujhe,
Yeh maine tay karliya.
Na ab unse koi mohabbat hai,
Aur na hi koi gila.
Bas yehi baat dil ko samjhane ki
Karrhi hu main sila.
Pagal thi, aur pagal hoon bas unke liye,
Par ab dil ko mana rahi hoon unko
Bhulne ke liye.

"Darkness Of My Life"

I was walking solely in the dark pavement/path,
And was waiting for someone to
Come and save me from death,
It was cloudy evening,
And I was roaming hither and thither
Since morning,
Tears were rolling down from eyes to cheeks,
But still didn't got none to wiped it out in peeks,
Was dieing poorly for someone's care,
And all had left me alone in fear,
How one can be so cruel?
Who once used to loved me eternally,
Now didn't have a speciality of being loyal,
Looking forward to the betrayal,
I literally accepted that love is just meant to fail,
Once you trap in the web of love,
You won't get free from this world of blur,
I literally need none in my house ward,
Just need few to come and visit in my graveyard.

KHEVANA PUROHIT

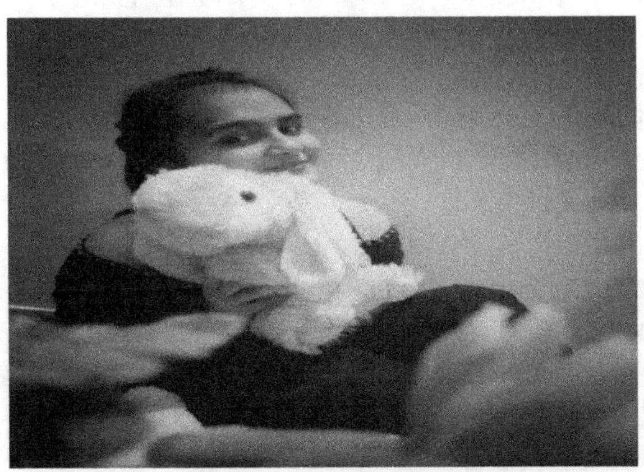

The co-author has just completed 12th science and now into Marwadi University for Information and Communication Technology. She writes articles, blogs, stories and poems with no professional experience. She is self made and passionate writer.

Betrayal

"Each betrayal begins with trust" – Martin Luther
This famous quote says that you ascend the stairs of betrayal when you convict.
Conviction is the plunge applied by us in being betrayed.
Whatever is the strude, there is no deck where you can reach without treachery.
In this epoch, everyone is meant to have affliction.
Whether it's your consociate, comrade, kin or relative, everyone has to evacuate.
But as we know, "Every collapse makes us get up again."
Betrayal is meant where you are concatenated.
We never get denounced by our rivals, they are the ones who adore, admire and acknowledge us.
But once you are conventioned with it, you get "Yourself".
You never get too much engaged and compassionate about anyone after that.
A person always learns from being deceived and anguished!
So make your betrayal your influence and live like you are the only one!

RIYA SRIVASTAVA

Poet by passion and entrepreneur by action. Writing is not only her passion but also to express her feelings. Follow her on Instagram@riyashrivastava2000

तेरा मुस्कुराना।
वो तेरा मुस्कुराना, नज़र यू झुकना
मुझे देख के यू तेरा बेवजह मुस्कुराना
दिल को चुराकर किया खुद से बेगाना
वो तेरा मुस्कुराना।
बातो से अपनी ओर बुलाना
नज़रो से यू घायल कर जाना
बिना जमाने की परवाह किये बिना
दिल की धड़कनों में सामना
वो तेरा मुस्कुराना।
जान ले कर यू अंजान बन जाना
आंखों से नींदों को चुराकर
सपनो में अपना बनाना
वो तेरा मुस्कुराना।

SRIYASRI PATRA

Sriyasri belongs to Rourkela of Odisha. She has completed her class 12 boards and is looking forward for a btech degree. She pours her heart out through writing. She speaks against anything that she finds inappropriate.

And it began with a robust greeting under the beautiful stars near the shore. My heart started beating faster and faster. My indefatigable loquacity went dumb to a dime. The sheer humbugs that I heard of him disappeared. I could feel a plethora of hormonal imbalances within. Everything inside me started fighting. My brain asked me to jump off and run away straight and eventually engaged in a quarrel with my heart that wanted all the clocks to stop ticking. And gradually his prudent eyes precluded me from running away. It became extremely difficult for me to decide of what I should do, due to the dissonance of my feelings. Everything is limpid but still, we were both nonplussed and gradually I started abhorring the idea of leaving the place and started enjoying the moment to the fullest. I turned fatuous and when he pulled me more towards him, forgetting everything, I fell in his arms and that's how our first date started.

GURLEEN KAUR

Her Name is Gurleen Kaur. She is born and brought up in Delhi. She is pursuing her graduation in tourism studies and french language. Her hobbies are writing, dancing and painting. She likes to express herself through words. She aspires to become a famous writer.

True Feelings

Understand my true feelings,
My inner wounds started healing.
The day I met you was my best,
Now please don't break my trust.
You see it as a friendship,
But if you see from my vision,
It's the most beautiful relationship.
Every moment was filled with magic ,
Day and nights were beautiful,
Now everything is tragic.
You don't understand anything,
Not even this thing,
That you have become my everything.
My love and my life,
You became the reason of me being alive.
Understand that only you are my love,
And it's my true feeling.

PRAGYA VERMA

Pragya Verma is born and raised in Prayagraj, Uttar Pradesh. She is currently pursuing Bachelor's in Computer Application. She is a poetess and a writer. She has done 60+ anthologies as a co-author and currently she's compiling her own anthology. You can follow her on Instagram: @wordsofpragya

Mine

The shower of your love,
The safety in your arms,
All these things are all of the above.
Your memories bring all of your charms.

Your pure heart, your true care,
You are someone I don't want to lose I swear.
Sweet, bitter, crazy memories with you,
Is something that will keep me always close to you.

No lies, no cries,
I only want to see your laughter and your smiles.
I hate that time when you are not around,
You healed me and recovered my wound.

The day i found you I will never forget,
I want you to be mine in every life I get.

SUPRABHAT

Serves under Central Government as Patent Examiner. Completed his graduation in Mechanical engineering. He developed a passion for creative writing from childhood. He loves to write fiction based on real life experiences. He inspires himself by meeting different people during solo-travel. He has keen interest in reading romance and relaxes himself by listening to music. Cooking acts as a stress buster for him. He is working on his full length romance-novel, which will be published in 2021.

His instagram handle: @bonjour_lekhak

Please Don't Cry!

Oh, God!
What erroneous had I done?
What agony had I given?
Why was my vexation not ending?
Why was 'my fear' not smiling?

Oh, God!
She has eyes, but couldn't discern;
She has ears, but couldn't listen.
'My fear' had lost her redolence;
But her aura wasn't any indifference.

Oh, God!
I could bear my pain, not hers;
She is not mine, can't help her.
Shiva, Please give me her pain,
And bring a smile on her face again!

PADMA SRIVASTAVA

She is a born writer, Padma Srivastava, born and brought up in Varanasi and started writing from the age of 13year. She is a student of Archaeology with it she is also a good writer and singer. She got this talent of composing music and poetry in inheritance. She always keeps very different way of thinking from people, she has a philosophical sight for everything. Philosophical from inside and nature lover from outside. She has been co _author of several anthologies.

बेपनाह पर अधूरा इश्क़ हमारा

मरती थी वो दिलों जान से मुझपे दौर था कुछ
ऐसा इश्क़ का, कि मैं भी सिर्फ उसपे ही फ़िदा था,
मेरी मंजिल थी किसी और गली को मुड़ती
कुछ पल को था मिला ज़रूर पर,
उसका रास्ता मुझसे बिल्कुल जुदा था
और कुछ यूं ही, अनकहे अहसासों से भरा
लफ़्ज़ों के बयान से परे मुझे अधूरा इश्क़ हुआ था
हां सुलझाता था वो जुल्फ़ों को मेरी और मैं
उसके बातों में कुछ उलझ सी जाती थी
कभी गुस्सा कभी बहकी यादों में उसके
बस कुछ यूं ही मैं अपनी मोहब्बत निभाती थी
कहा था किसी ने इन हाथ की लकीरों को देखकर
इश्क़ मिलेगा तो बेशक ज़िन्दगी में और
लकीरें भी ये साथ तो है पर हमारी नहीं
न मिले हम दोनों ही एक दूजे को शायद
किस्मत का पलड़ा भारी हुआ था
अब लकीरों पर तो कोई वश न था अपना पर हां
एक दफ़ा वो बेपनाह इश्क़ मुझे भी हुआ था।।

RAJVEER ATAL

He is Rajveer Atal from Gwalior currently he is a Medico. He gonna write his heart out. His aim is not to reach everyone but to some for sure. He writes on things that he sees, feel and experience.

He was also a part of Sanjivani public school Sabalgarh where he did teacher job for 1 year to fullfill his dreams as a teacher too, where he not only teaches children's but also learn from children's also. He loves children. He always motivates others for growing up according to him smart work really works if you wanted to be.

Negative

A secret that is dark...
Burns and tears the soul
But Gods too had their days...
Guilt is never an option

Respect is some chronic disease
Philosophy is close to catastrophe
The middle finger stands tall..
Against all fingers that are raised

Eighteen starts the mating
Time is just a waste of time
The eternal three magic words
Lose out to the three letter word

Music's always been personal
Every chord of that guitar
Resonates with fame and name..
Hidden beneath some rock star

Blood is thicker than water
But much thinner than alcohol
Insomnia is more an attitude...
Making the nights stand out...

A sin so blissful...
A truth so damn naked
Life floats on this smoke
Its dawn for the negative...

S. SARASWETHA

She is Saraswetha. She is pursuing her B.A.English degree. She is from Villupuram, Tamil Nadu. She likes to be familiar with everyone. She strongly believes that love supports life. She is fond of writing quotes and short stories in English.

Lines Of Adoration

•There are only two happiness in life:
To love and to be loved.

•Being in love gives more potential,
To face the hard times in our life.

•My soul, body and even memories are surrounded by you-
My love.
•My love for you will not be parallel,
It will inflate every day.

•When a journey ends, it means we return home.
But when our love ends, it means we won't return to our
normal life.

JACOB ROSARIO

He is Jacob Rosario of 17. He his currently pursuing his 12th STD. He is from Tindivanam. His ambition is to become "President of India". He is a Writer in a page of Instagram @quotes_from heartmaker. His dream is to Rule the Country. This is his debute book as a co-author. To contact him @jack_rio18 in Instagram.

INDIA

DEAR INDIANS,

''BEING A HUMAN IS GLORY TO OUR SOCIETY
BUT
BEING A SOLDIER IS A PRIDE OF OUR NATION''

INDIA is happy and safe because of our Indian Soldiers.
They dedicate their life for us. They sacrifice their Happiness
for us. They suppress their feelings for us.
We have many Religions many Caste many Culture many
Traditions but we all bonded in one thing, that is India. India
has a name and fame because of the Unity. India the other
name is Unity.

Indians have freedom but People used to misuse. Culprits
have to be punished hard.

"Crimes can be stopped
When
Laws becomes Unbreakable"

India is a Gift of every Indians. It has peace among Nation,
Friendship in the Countries.
Every Indian should learn the First thing which is
'Humanity'.

"Beauty shows your face,
Attitude shows your Talent,
Love shows your patience,
Friendship shows your character,
But
Heart only shows your

"Humanity"

India has a Lot of good stuff. Indians are Lovable. They are Respectful. They won't give up their rights. They will not give their Homeland for Anyone.

INDIA is a Construction of Family

'STUDENTS' are the Basement of India
'YOUNGSTERS' are the Pillars of India
'PARENTS' are the Workers of India
'SENIOR CITIZEN' is the Engineers of India

"DEAR INDIANS THIS IS NOT MY
WORDS,
IT'S MY FEELINGS"

SONA AGARWAL

The Young Emerging Author SONA AGARWAL is just 21 who is pursuing her graduation in the field of commerce, residing in Villupuram town within TamilNadu. She has done many anthologies and now doing her own one. She loves to enjoy the every moment of the life instead of doing or travelling in one path.

Dry Pain, Wet Love

Things passed by lot,
The love remained the same!
Why can't I be pinned?
At the heart of your life!

We fought a lot,
The smile remained the same!
Why can't this be finished?
At the depth of the sky!

We shared a lot,
The group of care remained the same,
Why can't it be forever?
At the sole property of us!

The understanding may lack,
The common things remained same,
Why can't we understand each other?
At the soul mirror of us!

KRISHNA MOTWANI

Krishna Motwani is a Student currently.
She is a moody girl.
She started writing in the month of june,2020.
She loves to write shayaris, small poems on love, family, friends, nature, and many more.
She writes in her free time.
She also writes some motivational quotes or poetries too and practices artworks also.
She lives her life like a bird
As bird flies freely and enjoys life like that she also lives her life freely and enjoy fullest.

करते एक दूसरे से खूब प्यार,
पर किया नहीं इज़हार।

एक को चोट लग जाए,
तो दूसरे की सास अटक जाए।

एक दिन दोनों मिले बगीचे में,
बताया एक दूसरे को, था जो दिल में।

घर में बताया दोनों ने,
ना की बड़ी आवाज़ पड़ी सुनने।

कुछ दिन दोनों रहे दूर,
मगर था दोनों में प्यार का सुरूर।

कई दिन बाद मिले दोनों छुपके से,
करते दोनों एक दूसरे से बहुत प्यार पर होना नहीं चाहते थे दूर घर
वालों से।

घर में बात मनाने कि फिरसे कोशिश की,
चमत्कार हुआ क्यूँ कि इस बार घर वालों ने हाँ की।

खुशी के मारे झूम उठे दोनों,
जैसे पंछी को पिंजरे से आज़ादी मिली जानो।

कुछ दिन बाद बस गया घर दोनों का,
जैसे पिछले जनम का रिश्ता हो अनोखा।

साथ निभाएँगे ये वादा किया,
अकेला ना छोड़ेंगे वो ठान लिया।

गए दोनों एक दिन कही घूमने,
धक्का दिया लड़की को पानी में किसने।

लड़के ने ढूँढा बहुत उसे,
अपना दर्द बताया नहीं किसीसे।

लड़की को खोने से रो पड़ा वो,
चोट लगी बहुत बड़ी उसके दिल को।

करता वो आज भी उससे बहुत प्यार,
करता नहीं अपने दुख का इज़हार।

MONISHA. T

She was originally from Thiruvannamalai (Erumpundi)
But she is currently lived in Villupuram. She is 18 years of age.
There will be a deeper concept in all of her poems. The
Decisions she makes will all be better. She will keep everyone in
 Balance. She will never leave her family for anything or anyone
 In life. She always motivates others.
Twitter: Monisha.T

Search Bar..!

The first girlfriend everyone got in life was her
Mother and the boyfriend was her Father…!
There is no one in this world
If there are no recipients..;
So everyone choose another person to
Feel her Mother's love and Father's protection
For the second time in her life..;
Such a quest can be called a Love..!
There is no age and no end to search and
Love is just like that…!
We need a hand to help us to cross the difficult path of life
We have love as a search bar to find that hand..;
Lovers may die but love never dies… it's a feeling..!
Love is like a tidal sea that never stops..!

KATHIJATHUL KUBRA. R

She is Kathijathul kubra who is 19 pursing her degree in the field of commerce and residing in TamilNadu. She is found of priceless things. Her love for others will be constant. She is a unique person who stays odd. She strongly believe god. She starts to convey her feeling of love through words. The words are written in her own

Twitter: 79andampully kubra

There are many people in this world
But I choose you
There are many shoulders to lay
But I need yours
There are many people to care
But I'm fond of yours

When you stand by my side
The total amount of blessing is showers on me
Nothing can make me happy
Than your shinning laugh

While in the days of my absence
You fulfilled with our memory
There are thousands of feelings
But your feelings is my every time favourite
Your hug made me to stand stronger
Your days are unforgettable
Which we can't replace
-Friendship

YASMIN. S

She has a Graceful and Sophisticated yet simple charm. She will make you laugh in the hardest time because she loves to see people happy. Her smile is infectious and she laughs all the time which everyone loves about her. She is 19 years old. She is the one and only YASMIN.

Every heart sings a Song late at night,
Some dare to write, while
Some bleed through their EYES.
Forgetting someone
You loved is like a Hell,
She forgive, but she won't forget.
Yes it's tough to Think,
But it's too hard to forget.
Facing the worst hurtings,
But still won't give up.
The day I'll stop loving you is the day,
The rivers make the sea to overflow.
I don't know who am I , but
When tears are in my Eyes,
I know I'm still Alive to write,
what is burning me inside.!
If I had nothing but I had you ,
I would have Everything.
It's unworthy for those who went up!
I wanna be the Last and Only one
You Loved.
Thou it's hard for you to understand the
 LOST SOUL.

LENA. M

Her sweet name was Lena. She thank her parents for encouraging her. This poem was very special to her because she loved to be smiling always. She loves nature.

Smile

Best medicine ever founded!
Even I was in pain, I used to smile!
But why? Because it make me to feel better!
A smile from my teacher gives me a confidence!
A smile from my love gives me a unique feel!
A smile from my friend gives me a funny memory!
A smile from a begger when I donate him some money,
Gave me a mixed feeling of happiness and sadness!
A smile from a child when I bought her a toy, gave me a best
way to start my day!
Smile is the best makeup you can wear!
Make a mask of smile on your face!
Then you will be the most needed person,
For the people around you!

DHRUVI DHARIWAL

Dhruvi Dhariwal, a 15 year old girl from Raipur Chhattisgarh who is very passionate about writing and sports. She is very sincere toward her work. She has a million dreams and is working on them. Whatever she dreams she does it.

Love is a medicine which heal all the wounds

SOFIYA MEHAKE N

Sofiya Mehake was born in Mysore but was brought up in Tindivanam. By this year she found her love for Hindi poetry.
Instagram handle- sprinkling_sparking_words

Jahaan-E-Ishq

Ishq Kiya hai Maine,
Bepanah Kiya hai,
Koi gunaah Nahi kiya.
Jahaan-e- ghum ko Bhula Diya
Kyunki doob Gaye tere ishq mein
Samaj naa Aaya Kuch   hogaye the hum paagal tere
ishq mein
Tere bepanaah ishq ne Kiya hame mashoor
Teri doori ne Kiya hame choor choor
Tha mujhe intezaar ki koi kare mujhe pyar
Naa chode Mera haath
Hui meri dua qubool
Aur Mila tera Saath...

KOWSALYA THANGADURAI

Kowsalya Thangadurai loves Literature. Currently she is pursuing Bachelors degree in Literature (B.A). She is very fond of writing poems, skits, etc; Apart from writing she is interested in sports.

Ig: kowsidurai14

LIFELINES
Live your life the way you love,
Love your way which you live.
Your life is only yours.

WANT U FOREVER
It is easy to say no one is permanent,
But, very hard to accept when it comes to you.

YOU ARE MINE
I may not be your first love,
But, I swear
I will be your best love.

ADVENTUROUS LIFE
You will feel your life is an adventure, when you want to get
married your beloved with your parents support.

THAT SOMEONE
I treated you as my soul, but you proved I'm just your pal.
I thought you are my whole life, but u proved I'm just a part
of your life.

SUJISH KANDAMPULLY

Being a graduate in Electrical Engineering and a passionate Writer, Sujish is also a Nutritionist, Blogger, Author, Photographer & a Philanthropist. He is recognized as an International Poet on Poetry Soup which is world's largest community of international poets.

He is also the author of the book "Soul Strings" published by Yourquote. Most of his works are based on his personal life experiences. Sujish has taken a deep dive into the ocean of life where he goes in search of understanding the core importance of a human's life and their journey based on which he has come up with some really wonderful & touching masterpieces. His motive is to help make people's life better by spreading positivity through his writings. You can find his work on platforms like Yourquote and Writco.

To receive a constant stream of motivation & inspiration from his work, you can follow him on his Instagram page @sujish_kandampully_official. To get in touch with him, shoot a mail to sujish92@gmail.com.

Our Last Fight

I'm weeping every night,
I'm missing you every night,
I'm thinking of you every night,
As I loved you with all my might.

I know it is too late
To make things alright,
Your dreams disturb me all the time
Whenever I try to sleep at night.

I wish I got a chance
To see your small sight,
As I think of you tonight
I could hug my pillow tight.

Since the time you have gone
Every second thought of yours,
Have brought tears in my eyes
I won't give up now without one more fight!

A Love Quote for Her

There is nothing happier than spending my whole life cuddling and loving you.

YASH OJHA

He is "YASH OJHA" son of 'Dr. Ram Sahay Ojha' and 'Mrs. Usha Ojha', born and raised in Ayodhaya, UP. He completed his schooling from Udaya Public School and now is pursuing Graduation in Arts (hons.) with English currently. He has a Degree in Hacking field as well. Writing was not a profession but somehow became passion for him. Now he has completed his own 30+ Poetries as well. The flow of his words seemed effortless, and before he knew about it. It had grown beyond this much poetry which was on his hands.

He received so much encouragement and positive feedbacks from his parents and others and then he found that he shouldn't stop writing.

"Relationship At A Glances"....

Relationships are the spice of life which contains love of Emotions, Feelings between the LOVEBIRDS till survival;

Relationship make two hearts feel alive in a way that no one can do anything else can;

Relationship can be Genuine when two people show that they care for each other, and there should be full confidence believe between them without any ego clashes;

Relationship between the LOVEBIRDS with understanding of both sides can make a big act of love and affection;

Relationship should feel loved and cared for when they know that their significant other is thinking about how to give them the most Pleasure and best ever Smile on their faces;

"Relationship is the key to keeping the LOVEBIRDS closer and together and flying at higher peak without any break";

Without these, any relationship will soon lose its way to shine....

PRAGYAN PANDA

Pragyan is perusing her B.Tech in "Chemical Engineering" from IGIT, Sarang. She's a short girl from Rourkela, Odisha. With fascination of nature, she's a spiritual person who motivates people. She does weird stuff like interacting with non living ones and pens down her mind. For more of her works, do follow her IG @quote_love_97.

Purple Royalty

As the rarest of royal luxury;
The unique purple in nature and crowned queen's entity.
It is when we ain't giving up to compromises till ultimate perfection;
The phonemes to the garrulous addiction.
The scents of the corpse flower;
Yes, royalty emerges beyond power.

LOVE'S MAGIC SIGNAL

The cheering days and sleepless nights_
It's love and it's happy sights.

The best experiences of body, mind and soul;
Are the love's ultimate goal.

The best ever fantasy becomes reality:
This is love's virtuality.

The addiction, the sensation and the soothing
Clings to brains as the best satisfaction.

Even then if you are shy to confess;
There comes situation of ecstasy to witness.

DIKSHA MOTWANI

Diksha Motwani is a moody girl. She loves to pen her thoughts. She is mostly introvert but her pen makes her extrovert.

Sleepless Nights.

Groaning on my bed,
Old chats I read,
I was full of tears,
For losing you, I always fears,
Most I loved,
More I cried,
Left alone with my broken heart,
All of it was your love art.

NIHAL. M. JAGIRDAR

She is Nihal from city called Vijayapura in Karantaka.Her
life lessons have inspired her to pen it down to express it. She
is writing since she was 12. Besides writing she is pursuing
her degree in computer science engineering.

My Journey

An early sunny morning, when the cold wind sings.
My mother in labour brought me to the world.
It was the day of nov.
Everyone's face with smile and heart full of bliss.
And me with full of cheery cry.
I was nurtured with love, care and affection,
Which made me matured one today?
Relying on everything on everyone started to do my duty on the Way.
I have seen many ups and downs, crusts and troughs through which I fall and rise.
Learned from selfish world, which made me braver and stronger.
I am the elder to take my siblings on the way of happiness and success.
I pray almighty that my dreams to be my goals and goals to be my future ahead.

JATA_V

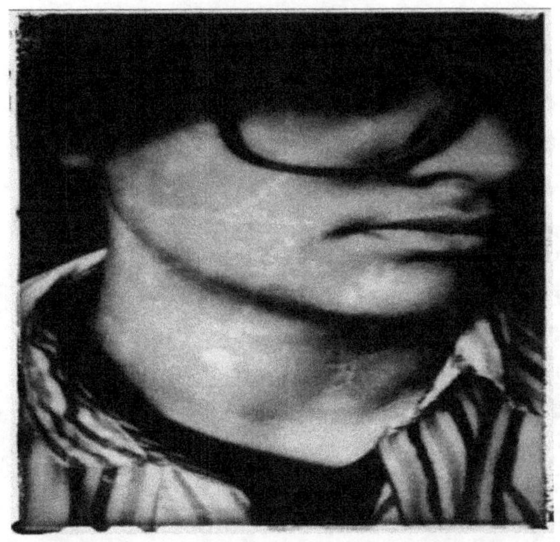

Jata_V, an instrument of Nature, existing in the Indian subcontinent. Time's person of the year 2006, Jata doesn't have a heart of its own. Alien to selfish Love and fellow human expressions. Currently moonwalking at the tributary where fantasy stream merges with roller coaster life.

Wine Is Red But Also Is Blood...

As rare as Golden Blood,
I found this Innocence in this girl.
As unknown as a diamond out of dirt,
I didn't recognize it at first.
I remember how she confessed
Her love in the most innocent manner.
Still, I've never ever admitted
That I too loved her as the same.
In the beginning, I might have just attracted
Just for her beauty, I didn't know me then!
As days pass by, I noticed that,
This Love on her slowly augmented...
Listening to her ballad every day,
My rains and roses were just blasted!
All I thought is that I found this Innocence,
In a true companion with whom I could
Spend my entire life with...just ecstasy!
Until that day when she abruptly concluded
The chapters of Innocence and Truth...
Breaking my rarest trust in her, she cheated!
She said, "Since I love you, I want you to be my slave forever!"
I regretted my wrong choice of trusting her, my heart exploded...
With her love drama, she just proved to me that,
"No Innocence And No True Love Exist In This World!"

JAPSIMRAN KAUR

A 22 year old girl, Japsimran Kaur belongs from Punjab. She has recently completed her graduation in Education from Punjab University, Chandigarh and pursuing masters in Punjabi. She aspires to become a good teacher and make learning interesting.

Simply sweet and beautiful girl, she's a studious and a religious person. She has been recently a part of the anthologies 'Diary of Emotions', 'Bandhan Rishto Ke' and 'Voice of the Souls' as a Co-Author. She always initiate to participate in different activities and in organize of various events.

She believes that everyone is not the perfectionist in their life but can learn to be that from every part of nature and life lessons. She wants to explore and learn her whole life as she believes that there is no age limit for learning. She always wants to do and achieve best of everything for her and her family. She is not a professional writer, simply just pen out her feelings and emotions through quotes and poetry.

She can be contacted at her-

Instagram Page - @artforlife1998

Facebook Page - ART for LIFE

My Angel

My little girl, my Angel
Here on earth without wings
I love you so much
You're a part of me
In so many ways

Not only my niece,
Not just my best friend
I love you like a sister and daughter
And always will, with no end

It's my job to protect you
And look after you forever
You'll always be my baby
Even when you're big enough

You have no idea how much happiness you truly brings
You brightens up my days with your smiles and laughs
You helps me to remember all the blessings that I have
Your face, it is so perfect, you're sweet and soft and pure
You give the greatest hugs from morning until night.

रेत पर लिखा था कुछ

रेत पर लिखा था कुछ,
जिंदगी के वो गम जो किसी को कह ना सके,
सोचा शायद कोई तो उसे पढ़कर समझेगा,
मगर हवा का झोंका अपने साथ ही वो सारे गम उड़ा ले गया।

PRATHAM MITTAL

He is very Positive, kind, helpful, friendly and happy soul. His passion is painting and writing. He has won many competitions, He has Been Co-Authored of 55+ Anthology and He has Been Compiler of 10+ Anthologies, and in the Process for more. He is an OMG Books Of Record Holder + Bravo International Book of World Record Holder for his Anthology Speaking My Truth. Participated in International Writing Competitions and Featured in Many Magazines also.

"So many of our dreams at first seem impossible, then they seem improbable, and then, when we summon the will, they soon become inevitable."

RUMA BEGAM

Hello myself Ruma Begam... Post graduate..
So simple & positive minded girl..
Passionate writer...
Photography, painting and writing is my hobby...
Am also fond of reading...
I like to travel...misleading people is the best part of my life.... Talkative but with in my comfortable zone... I have written in many anthologies & am aslo compiling a new anthology.
Instagram Handle: pachu338
Mail: rumabegam1996@gmail.com

तूने मुजे धोखा नहीं दिया

खोया नहीं हूं पेयार में, अभी यादे जिंदा हैं।
तो क्या हुआ वो नहीं हैं मेरे पास, जितना पेयार मिला उसमें खुश हूं
में।।

आरे दिल टूटा हुआ तो क्या, मुजे तन्हा कर वी गया तो क्या....
मुजसे बिछार कर उसने, यह दिल खुदा से जोर गया।।

हाँ पेयार बेशुमार हैं तूजसे अभी वी, पर तूजे पाने की तमन्ना नहीं
हैं....
हाँ पेयार बेशुमार हैं तूजसे अभी वी, पर तूजे पाने की तमन्ना नहीं
हैं....
तेरे
तेरी जमीन को मेरी पेरु ताले रख कर देखा हैं मैँ ने, जो तूने किया
वो वी सही हैं।।

मजबूरी सबकी अलग अलग हैं, हान बयान वी तूने हजार बार
किया....
खुश हूं में यह सोच कर की मजबूरी थी तेरी, तूने मुजे धोका तो
नहीं दिया।।

दिल टूटा ही सही, जुबान खामोश ही सही, खुदा ने इस दिल को
सूकून से भर दिया....
शुकर गुजार हूं तेरा बोहत में, कि तूने लरखाराते जूवान को
खामोशी से भर गाया।।

पर तूने मुजे धोखा नहीं दिया।

उम्मीद दोबारा जग ऊटी हैं, जब तूने लोट आया।
मासूम इस दिल को, फिरसे खुशी से भार गाया।।

इसबार सपने अलग दिखाई तूने, भरोसा फिरसे दिलाया।
खामोश इस चेहरे पर, फिरसे एक मुस्कान हैं लाया।।

शिकायत हजारों की तुझसे, छोर जाने की सारे दुख बतलाया।
दुख तेरी दिल पर वी था, उदास चेहरे से ये वी समझाया।।

लोट आने की खुशी में, जब में रातभर रोया।
इस पागल से मुलाकात के खातिर, दौरा चला आया।।

खामोश मेरी जुबान थी, आखों में शिकायतौ की ढेर था।
फिरसे पिगली तेरी पेयार में, ना जाने बातो में कौनसी जादू था।।

बताया सारी परिसानी मेरी, तू सुनके खामोश राहा।
फिरसे चला गया दूर मुझसे, छोरके मुजे अकेला वहाँ।।

बताया तेरी मजबूरी मुजे, फिरसे वादा करके छोर गाया।
साथ ना निभाया तूने मेरी, बीच सड़क में रोला दिया।।

था मजबूरी तेरी सच्चा ही, दिल चाकना चूर कर गाया, फिरभी
बोलती हूं में सनाम, तूने मुजे धोका नहीं दिया।।
तूने मुजे धोखा नहीं दिया ।

-IPSITA PANIGRAHI

A carefree, joyful, realistic in practical life but she enjoys to live in an imaginative and fictional world. This is Ipsita Panigrahi, a budding writer, who loves to express her feelings and emotions through writings. She hails from Bhubaneswar -the city of temples, Odisha. She has a passion for literature, as she loves to do all those stuff which makes her happy and literature is one among them. She is likely to be called as a scribbler. She finds peace in gardening and reading books and an artist is also hidden in her.

The Dark...Yet Spark...!!!

When I look into the dark.
Everything around is black,
But my soul can feel the spark.

The spark of positivity in negativity.
The flicker of creativity in illusions.
I calm myself,
I sit with silence.
And can hear the sound of lark.

Everything becomes stable.
And I find myself different from the rabble.
I get my answers of my confusions.
Which where unanswered due to delusion?

Flairs and Glairs, a platform by a student for the students. We are esteemed youth struggling to carve out our path for our future and we follow a basic mindset Since everyone is not born with all-round skills. Joining hands with people who are born to execute it with perfection is the best way to evolve. Self-Evolution is the need of the hour but, evolving as a community is what we strive for. The initiative as kickstarted by, Founder- Mr. Shubham Shah with the motive to utilize the skillset and talent of writing has now a team of 10+ people who are actively participating into newer forms of learning and discovering talents among youngsters. We Provide platform and services like Publishing opportunities, Open mics, Workshops, Hands-on training. Operating with Brand Name of Flairs and Glairs (Publication House), we offer the chance of elevating a passionate writer to an esteemed author With Brand name Teekhe Zasbaaat. We bring to you an opportunity to get accustomed with the Public Speaking and Presenting of Thoughts along with regular challenges to brush up your inking spirit. The newest initiative to extend our services we introduced in a new writing Platform- The Glittering Fables and Ink Over Tears.

We Choose to Fly Like A Falcon than to be

a Leg Pulling Crab.

To Know More: Infoline – 7781900870
Mail Us At-
flairsandglairs@gmail.com / info@flairsandglairs.in
Or Visit is at
www.flairsandglairs.com / www.flairsandglairs.in
Social Handles- @flairsandglairs @teekhezasbaaat

www.ingramcontent.com/pod-product-compliance
Lightning Source LLC
Chambersburg PA
CBHW061237140726
47998CB00006B/2019